GW00809200

Colette Robinson was born and raised in Belfast, Northern Ireland where her love of storytelling was ingrained in her from a young age.

She now resides in Sydney, Australia and is an avid reader, writer and booklover!

Please follow Colette on Instagram: https://www.instagram.com/robinsonreads8/

Bessie Beam from Brayfoot Cottages

© 2023 Colette Robinson. Illustrations © 2023 Jess Bircham. Layout Simon Creedy

All rights reserved. No part of this book may be reproduced or transmitted in any form or by any means, electronic or mechanical, including photocopying, recording, or by any information storage and retrieval system, without written permission from the author.

ISBN 978-0-6458749-0-7

For

Ray

BESSIE BEAM
FROM BRAYFOOT COTTAGES

Written by Colette Robinson
Illustrated by Jess Bircham

Bessie Beam and Mr Picklebottom

At the bottom of Fairy Lane, in a row of cottages, lives Bessie Beam.

Fairy Lane is magical. It is filled with fairies who have lived here for thousands of years. The fairies have beautiful big wings with bright colours. Bessie Beam loves living in Fairy Lane.

Bessie is best friends with Nellie, Zara and Daisy, three of the child fairies. They love to play games, dance and sing together.

Fairy Nellie has bright yellow wings, Fairy Daisy's wings are deep purple and Fairy Zara has pale pink ones, which just happens to be her favourite colour.

Bessie is the only person who can see and hear the fairies. Sometimes the adults think Bessie is talking to herself when she is chatting with them.

Bessie and the fairies have a special secret code. Two big CLAPS. So, if Bessie wants the fairies, she just claps her hands twice above her head.

CLAP! CLAP!

All the other fairies sleep under the bushes in the gardens of Fairy Lane but Fairies Nellie, Zara and Daisy sleep at the bottom of Bessie's bed.

This afternoon when Bessie was playing hopscotch with Fairies Nellie and Daisy, Fairy Nellie said, "I am a little worried about Mr Picklebottom in Cottage No. 4, he was looking very sad this morning."

"Oh dear, let's go check he's okay," said Bessie.

"Hello? Anyone home?" called Bessie.

Mr Picklebottom opened the door looking very sad. "Oh, Mr Picklebottom, what's wrong?" asked Bessie.

Mr Picklebottom is a very tall man with very long legs. He has no hair and wears tiny black glasses right on the tip of his nose.

"Oh Bessie, I have lost Rodney again! I can't find him. I have looked everywhere."

Rodney is Mr Picklebottom's dog. He is black and white and very fluffy and always getting up to mischief. He loves playing hide and seek and hides in the strangest places.

"It's okay Mr Picklebottom, I will look for him," said Bessie.

Bessie and the fairies look under the bed, on top of the wardrobe, and in the washing machine.

The fairies sprinkle their magical wishing dust everywhere, and as they sprinkle it, they make a wish, one to find Rodney.

Suddenly, Bessie sees a little head popping up and down at the window of the garden shed.

It's Rodney!

Rodney has fallen into a box and isn't able to get out. He is jumping up and down hoping someone will see him.

"Mr Picklebottom, I found Rodney," called Bessie.

"Oh Rodney, you naughty dog, you gave me
such a fright," said Mr Picklebottom.

Rodney is so happy he can't stop licking
Mr Picklebottom's face.

Bessie looks in the box where Rodney was hiding.
There are lots of beautiful paintings.

"I'm throwing out all this rubbish, I painted those when
I was a young man, I'm a silly old fool for keeping them,"
said Mr Picklebottom.

Bessie Beam has an idea. She rushes off with
the paintings to talk to her neighbours.

That night Bessie and the fairies are
so excited they can barely sleep!

The next day Bessie arrives at Mr Picklebottom's
garden. Mr Tum is hanging all the paintings in
colourful frames from the branches of the trees,
with fairy lights all around.

It is a beautiful mini art gallery. The fairies dance with delight. All the neighbours start to arrive. Mrs Hector arrives with lemonade and Dr Stanley with balloons.

Bessie Beam is beaming from ear to ear.

Bessie knocks on Mr Picklebottom's door.

"Good Morning Mr Picklebottom,
it's Bessie, can you please come out?"

Mr Picklebottom opens the door.
"Oh, my goodness me," he says.

Everyone is clapping and cheering for
Mr Picklebottom and his amazing artwork.

"I am the happiest man on the planet and it is
all thanks to Bessie Beam. First she found
Rodney and then my old paintings."

The fairies and Bessie dance in the garden. They are delighted the magical wishing fairy dust worked, Rodney was found and Mr Picklebottom is a very happy man.

The End

Bessie Beam and the Bunnies

Bessie Beams jumps quickly
out of bed.

"Oh my, oh my, I think I must have slept
in this morning! It's so bright, it must be
lunchtime." Bessie runs to the window
and pulls open her blinds.

WOW!

What a wonderful sight! The sun is shining
brightly with not a cloud in the sky.

It had been raining all week and the sky had
been dark and gloomy. Bessie is excited that
today she can go outside to play again.

CLAP! CLAP!

Fairies Nellie, Zara and Daisy appear. They are so happy, they like playing in the gardens in Fairy Lane. The gardens look beautiful when the sun shines and the flowers are in full bloom, which they are today. Each garden has so many colourful flowers it looks magical.

"Hurry up, hurry up Bessie, let's go outside, I want to dance in the garden," says Fairy Daisy. The fairies fly to the garden and Bessie runs after them. Zara and Nellie are dancing and twirling around. Daisy is happy trying out some new dance moves by herself.

"This is so much fun! Maybe we should make up a new dance routine," says Nellie.

"Oh yes, let's do that," says Zara.

Bessie Beam and the fairies are trying new dance moves when suddenly Bessie notices something moving behind the bushes.

Bessie peeks behind the bush. There are five baby bunny rabbits all huddled together. The baby bunnies are so cute and so small.

"Oh Bessie, where is their mummy?" asks Nellie. "They must be cold, should you bring them inside?"

Bessie calls to Mr Tum to come and have a look.

"Yes Bessie, we need to keep these bunnies warm until we can find their mummy. Can you help me make a bed for them?" asks Mr Tum.

Bessie and Mr Tum make a big bed out of a large cardboard box. Benny, Mr Tum's pet rabbit, is looking on thinking it might be for him.

Bessie fills the box with blankets and cuddly toys and places it next to Mr Tum's fire.

Bunny rabbits can run very fast and be very tricky to catch, but these bunnies are so small Bessie and Mr Tum are easily able to pick them up and carry them to their new bed. Mr Tum hums a little tune, and when they are all on the bed Bessie reads a story.

The baby bunnies nod off to sleep.

Benny is very curious. Hmmm, what are they
all doing in here? he thinks, but he really
doesn't mind as he likes the company.

That evening Bessie Beam and her mum go to visit the
bunnies. Mr Tum's door is open.

"Hello, anyone home?" calls Bessie.

As they push open the door, they are greeted with such
a funny sight! Mr Tum is on the floor playing with the
bunnies who are hopping all over the place. Fast asleep
in their bed is a big bunny.

"Oh, my goodness Mr Tum, is that their mum?
How did you find her?" asked Bessie.

"Well, I phoned the vet and told him about the baby
bunnies. He said just this morning a young woman
brought in a big bunny she had found. The bunny had a
sore paw, which the vet fixed up. He thought it might be
their mum so he brought her over right away.

The baby bunnies were so happy to see her.
They immediately had a big feed as they were so hungry.
The vet said it had to be their mum."

Bessie Beam is so happy the baby bunnies
have found their mum. Mr Tum will look after them all
until the big bunny's paw is completely better
and they can all go back outside.

Mrs Bunny and her babies have the best spot, beside the
fire. They are very comfortable with their special blankets.
Benny looks happy too as he cuddles up as well.

Outside it is just starting to get dark.

The lights in the houses on Fairy Lane are being
switched on. Bessie can see the pink, yellow and purple fairy
wings flying back to the garden. The fairies want to dance
just one more time before bedtime. Soon they will fly back to
Bessie's room and tuck themselves in at the bottom
of her bed, where they sleep every night.

Bessie Beam and Cuddles the Calf

Cuddles the Calf lives on
Farmer Davey's farm at the
top of Fairy Lane.

Cuddles the Calf loves to explore and is always getting lost. One day Farmer Davey found Cuddles in the pigs' pen, and another day he was beside Tiger the horse.

His mum Molly worries when Cuddles gets lost. Every morning Molly reminds him, "Cuddles, please do not wander off today and get lost." And every morning Cuddles the Calf says to himself, "Today is the day, Cuddles, that you will not get lost."

And every morning Farmer Davey checks Cuddles is with the other cows.

Today Farmer Davey is moving all
the cows to a new field.

Cuddles is walking closely beside his mum,
Molly. He is looking around and suddenly
notices some beautiful bright colours in the
sky, off in the distance. Cuddles thinks it might
be the fairies coming to visit him. He can see
and hear the fairies just like Bessie.

At that moment Farmer Davey opens the gates
and the cows walk quickly into the new field.

But Cuddles the Calf starts to walk in the
direction of the pretty colours, not into the
field, but right down Fairy Lane!

At the bottom of Fairy Lane Bessie Beam is flying her kite. She looks up and sees Cuddles the Calf walking towards her. Cuddles is so excited to see Bessie, she is his favourite human!

Cuddles can see the colours clearly now. It's not the fairies at all! How funny, Bessie is attached to the colours with a long piece of string, ah ha, it's a kite!

Well, he thinks, this is turning out to be quite an exciting day.

"Hello Cuddles, does your mum Molly know where you are?" asks Bessie.

Uh oh, I have got myself lost again, thinks Cuddles.

Back at the farm Molly is very sad and upset. Cuddles has gone missing again!

Bessie Beam needs some help from her best friends.
She puts her hands above her head,

CLAP! CLAP!

"Hello Cuddles," says Fairies Daisy and Zara.
Cuddles gives a big moo, "Hello."

"Can you help Cuddles get back to the farm?
Could you please find Farmer Davey?" asks Bessie.

"Yes please," says Cuddles.

Fairy Daisy and Fairy Zara are happy to help.
They fly off promising to be back soon.

Cuddles is getting tired now. It has been a long walk
down Fairy Lane. He is missing his mum and is upset
that he got himself lost again. He starts to cry.
Big fat tears roll down his face.

"Don't worry Cuddles, I will read you a story while
we wait," says Bessie.

Fairies Daisy and Zara fly as fast as they can to the farm.

They see Farmer Davey out looking for Cuddles,
so they fly right in front of him sprinkling magical
wishing dust, making a wish that Farmer Davey
finds the right way to Cuddles.

Can you believe it? Farmer Davey starts to walk
in the right direction, down Fairy Lane.

"Cuddles! There you are! You got lost again!
Goodness me, what am I going to do with you?"
asks Farmer Davey.

Cuddles jumps to his feet; he is so happy to
see Farmer Davey. Cuddles says to himself,
"I will never get lost again.
I will stay with Farmer Davey forever and ever."

Just then some new colours appear right in
front of Cuddles' nose. "Oh, I wonder what that
is?" thinks Cuddles. "Oh, so pretty and they
keep moving." Cuddles starts to follow.

Farmer Davey and Bessie Beam both shout out,

"Cuddles! STOP RIGHT THERE!"

33

Bessie goes to one side of Cuddles and
Farmer Davey goes to the other. They
walk him right back to Molly.

The fairies fly ahead sprinkling magical
wishing dust the whole way up Fairy Lane,
at the same time making fairy wishes for Cuddles
to keep walking in the right direction.

There is no chance Cuddles would get lost again!

The End

BESSIE BEAM AND THE FAMOUS MRS HECTOR

There is a very famous person
living in Fairy Lane. It is Mrs Hector.

Mrs Hector is famous for her beautiful baking.
She bakes magnificent cakes and buns.

She is so famous she has even been on
television showing people how to bake.

Mrs Hector also makes the best bread in
the country and amazing fruit scones.

Mrs. Hector loves to be in the kitchen baking,
it is her favourite room in her cottage.

Every morning at 6 o'clock, Mrs Hector begins baking. The fairies watch through the window. Rodney, Mr Picklebottom's dog, lies on Mrs Hector's kitchen floor hoping she will give him some when it's ready. Yum Yum.

Sometimes Bessie helps Mrs Hector to bake.

Mrs Hector loves to chat and sing while she bakes but yesterday, she wasn't very chatty at all. Bessie asked a question and Mrs Hector just didn't answer!

The fairies are having their morning tea and fairy bread with Bessie, when Fairy Zara asks, "Has anyone been around to Mrs Hector's cottage recently?"

"Oh yes, on Monday, I heard Mrs Hector
and Farmer Davey talking. Farmer Davey asked her
if would she like some eggs and Mrs Hector replied,
No thank you Farmer Davey, I do not want any pegs,
I have plenty of pegs," giggles Fairy Nellie.

"That's strange," says Fairy Zara.

"Yes, Farmer Davey looked very confused
and so did Mrs Hector," says Nellie.

"And just this morning I heard Mrs Hector talking to
Doctor Stanley," says Fairy Daisy.

Dr Stanley asked her, 'Mrs Hector, how is your
heart?' and Mrs Hector replied, 'Cart? You want a
cart? I'm very sorry Dr Stanley, I don't have a cart.
Most people these days don't use carts!'"

"That is also very strange. Let's go and see what Mrs Hector is doing now," says Fairy Nellie.

The fairies and Bessie Beam arrive together at Mrs Hector's cottage.

"Hello, Mrs Hector, how are you?" asks Bessie.

"What an awful thing to ask, Bessie, how's my poo? I will not be talking about that to anyone except Dr Stanley," replies Mrs Hector.

Bessie giggles. "Oh! Mrs Hector, did you not hear what I said?"

"What? You want to go to bed?" asks Mrs Hector.

Bessie keeps giggling and cannot stop.

She giggles and giggles so much she has
to lie down in the garden.

The fairies and Bessie are rolling on the grass
giggling, holding onto their tummies.
This looks like fun, thinks Rodney
and joins in as well.

Bessie notices a funny looking shiny object
under the rose bush. She reaches in and pulls it
out. It's Mrs Hector's hearing aid!

"Look, look Mrs Hector, I have
found your hearing aid."

Mrs Hector looks very surprised. She pops it in her ear and then she gets a fit of the giggles.

"That's why everyone sounded so funny," she says. "Thank you, Bessie, I thought everyone around here was going quite mad. I must say it did sound like everyone was talking underwater."

With her rolling pin tucked under her arm Mrs Hector goes back to her baking giggling to herself, "Oh I really need to turn down the television."

The fairies, Bessie and Rodney skip off to the bottom of the garden to play a game.

Whatever will happen next in Fairy Lane?
Such a fun place to live.

The End

BESSIE BEAM, MR TUM AND BENNY THE BUNNY

Mr Tum and Benny the Bunny love birthdays!

They organise all the birthday parties in Fairy Lane. This is a very important job. Mr Tum says it's the best job in the world.

He gets very excited planning the birthday cake, the balloons and the presents. For every party he dresses Benny in a big red party hat with tinsel strung all around his neck.

The fairies in Fairy Lane love the parties as well. Fairy Daisy loves to dance, and parties are the best place for that. Fairy Nellie sings along with the party music and flaps her beautiful yellow wings in time. Zara is the quietest of the fairies, she loves to just sit and watch all the people.

This morning Bessie Beam is playing just
outside Mr Tum's cottage.

CLAP! CLAP!

Fairies Daisy, Zara and Nellie come out to play.
They want to play hide and seek. Zara squeezes her
eyes shut tight while Nellie and Daisy fly off to hide.

Zara counts out loud, "One, two, three, four, five,
ready or not, here I come!"

Bessie loves watching the fairies play hide and seek.
As they hide behind the bushes Bessie can see their
colourful wings poking out. As Fairy Zara looks in the
garden, she glances up to Mr Tum's window.

She can see a big calendar on his wall and flies closer. The calendar has red circles around the dates of everyone's birthday.

Mrs Hector's birthday is May 1 and Bessie Beam's is October 26.

There are two birthdays in August, Farmer Davey and Mr Picklebottom's. Mr Tum organises an even bigger party in August. Two birthdays together are extra fun.

Fairy Zara looks again and notices a big red circle around last Saturday. There was no party last Saturday in Fairy Lane, thinks Fairy Zara.

"OH, MY GOODNESS ME!" she says aloud. "It was MR TUM's birthday last week, but he didn't give himself a party and he didn't even tell anyone."

Fairy Zara calls out, "Everyone, stop hiding, I need to talk to you." They come out right away. Bessie, Nellie and Daisy listen closely to Zara and come up with a plan.

The fairies fly away and Bessie goes to find Mrs Hector. Mrs Hector hears what is happening and starts baking a big birthday cake while Bessie makes a card for everyone in Brayfoot Cottages to sign.

This evening Mr Tum is giving Benny some carrots when he hears a noise outside. "Oh Benny, I wonder what that is, I will go and have a look."

Mr Tum opens his door and EVERYONE starts to sing.

"Happy Birthday to you...
Happy Birthday to you...
Happy Birthday dear
Mr TUUUUMMMMMM...
Happy Birthday to you!"

Mr Tum is so happy! Mrs Hector and Farmer Davey are holding the cake and Cuddles the Calf is trying very hard not to blow out the candles as he moos along in tune.

The fairies sprinkle their magical wishing dust over Mr Tum. People always make wishes when they blow out their birthday cake candles, and the fairies want to make sure Mr Tum gets whatever he wishes for.

Bessie Beam gives Mr Tum his birthday card. "Oh Bessie, that is just what I wished for... I have never had a birthday card in my whole life and I have always wanted one."

Mr Tum now has the biggest card and the most beautiful birthday cake he has ever seen. It was just magical.

Magic definitely happens when you live in Fairy Lane.

The End

Bessie Beam and
Doctor Stanley

Bessie Beam is not feeling very
happy today. In fact, she is
feeling quite strange.

When she woke up Fairy Nellie was perched
on the edge of her pillow.

"Oh Bessie, you must go see Dr Stanley, you really
don't look very well," said Fairy Nellie.

Dr Stanley is Fairy Lane's doctor. He lives in the end
cottage with a long pink bench under the window
where patients wait to see him.

Dr Stanley has very curly, bright red hair and large
round glasses. He carries a big black doctor's bag
full of medicines. Sometimes the fairies put some
magical medicines in his bag as well.

Bessie Beam and her mum go to see Dr Stanley. But when they arrive, they get a big shock.

The surgery is closed. "Oh my, I wonder why it's closed? Dr Stanley is always open," says Bessie.

Bessie's mum peeks in the window. Dr Stanley
is lying on his sofa looking very unwell.
His nose is bright red, almost the same colour
as his hair, he is coughing and spluttering
and his nose is running.

He tries to speak but instead sneezes
so hard that the fairy sitting on his
chair is blown sky high!

Dr Stanley is very sick. The fairies have
sprinkled their fairy magical wishing dust all
around Dr Stanley and are wishing him to get
well. Their magic always works, but this time
it is taking just a little bit longer.

Bessie and her mum go inside to try to help Dr Stanley. Bessie flops into his comfortable armchair, she is so tired herself, she decides to bring some extra help.

Bessie claps for the fairies.

CLAP! CLAP!

She whispers into Fairy Zara's ear. Zara, with her long pink wings, flies off to get help organised.

A few minutes later Mrs Hector arrives with her bucket and broom.

"Everything must be spick and span when someone is sick, I will start cleaning right away," she says.

Mr Tum arrives next with juice and water.

"Everyone must drink lots of fluids when they are sick," he says.

Mr Picklebottom and Rodney are next to arrive. "Everyone must rest when they are sick, so we have brought you some movies to watch," he says.

Then Farmer Davey and Cuddles the Calf pop their heads through the window. Farmer Davey says, "Hello, we heard you weren't feeling well, so we brought some vegetables from the farm."

"MOOOOOO," says Cuddles.

By the afternoon Dr Stanley is starting to feel much better. The fairies have been sprinkling their fairy dust in Dr Stanley's curly hair and right under his red nose. It is starting to work its magic! Bessie Beam is feeling better too.

The next morning Dr Stanley is ready to get back to work. He opens the door for his first patient, "Oh my goodness, look at everyone waiting!"

The **first** patient is Bessie Beam's mum!

The **second** patient is Mrs Hector!

The **third** patient is Mr Picklebottom!

The **fourth** patient is Farmer Davey!

Poor Cuddles the Calf is also unwell.

Everyone is sneezing and coughing with bright red noses.

There is only one thing he can do. He brings everyone inside.

Dr Stanley gives out some medicine while
Bessie hands out some water.

Fairy Daisy and Fairy Nellie are sprinkling a new batch
of magical wishing dust and whispering get well wishes
until everyone falls asleep.

When they wake up, they are feeling so much better. The
magical wishing dust, as well as the fairy wishes, have
worked their magic.

Everyone in Brayfoot Cottages thinks Dr Stanley is the
best doctor in the world. They say that Dr Stanley might
even be a bit magical or have magic in his medicine
because they all are feeling so good now.

The fairies and Bessie giggle when they hear this. If only
they knew that magic really does happen in Fairy Lane.

The End

THANK YOU FOR VISITING!
FROM ALL YOUR FRIENDS AT BRAYFOOT COTTAGES.

Printed in Australia
Ingram Content Group Australia Pty Ltd
AUHW012055091023
384705AU00001B/1